THIS WALKER BOOK BELONGS TO:

_____

_____

_____

*For
Emily and Daniel
M.W.*

*For
Joe and Sam
B.F.*

First published 2000 by Walker Books Ltd
87 Vauxhall Walk, London SE11 5HJ

This edition published 2001

10 9 8 7 6 5 4 3

Text © 2000 Martin Waddell
Illustrations © Barbara Firth

The moral rights of the author and illustrator
have been asserted.

This book has been typeset in Columbus.

Printed in China

British Library Cataloguing in Publication Data:
a catalogue record for this book is available from the British Library.

ISBN 978-0-7445-8280-2

www.walkerbooks.co.uk

Tom Rabbit

Martin Waddell

illustrated by

Barbara Firth

WALKER BOOKS
AND SUBSIDIARIES
LONDON • BOSTON • SYDNEY • AUCKLAND

One summer evening
Tom Rabbit and Sammy
went out to the back field
to see the real rabbits.

Tom Rabbit and Sammy
climbed up on the wall.

"We can see the whole world
from here," Sammy said
to Tom Rabbit.

"I'm happy with Sammy,"
Tom Rabbit thought.

Then Harry came by the back field with the cows, and Sammy ran off to help Harry.

Tom Rabbit was left all alone on the wall.

"Sammy won't be gone long," thought Tom Rabbit.

Mum called Sammy in
for his supper, and Sammy
went into the house.

"I hope Sammy comes back,"
thought Tom Rabbit.

The sun set on the field
and the moon rose.

"I've not seen that before,"
thought Tom Rabbit.

And then,
from the bank
at the end of the lane
the wild rabbits came ...

first one

and then two

and then three

and then four

and then more.

Wild rabbits were there,
everywhere ...

everywhere that
Tom Rabbit could see.

"I wish Sammy was here,"
thought Tom Rabbit.

A rabbit hopped up on the wall.
It quivered its nose
at Tom Rabbit.

"It's only a rabbit the same as
I am," thought Tom Rabbit.
"I'm not scared
one bit."

The light went on in Sammy's
bedroom. Tom Rabbit saw
it shine over the field.

"Sammy won't go to bed without
me," thought Tom Rabbit.

"Sammy can't go to bed without
me," thought Tom Rabbit.

The light went out
in Sammy's bedroom.

"Sammy's gone to bed without
me," thought Tom Rabbit.
"I'm all alone now."

And that's when …

Sammy came back
for Tom Rabbit.

"I'm sorry I left you,
Tom Rabbit," said Sammy
and he carried Tom Rabbit
back home.

Tom Rabbit and Sammy
got into bed.

"Goodnight Sammy,"
said Mum. "And goodnight
Tom Rabbit."

"Goodnight Mum,"
said Sammy.

"I'm happy with Sammy,"
Tom Rabbit thought,
and he snuggled down
safe in bed beside Sammy.

Other titles by Martin Waddell and Barbara Firth

ISBN 978-1-84428-491-7

ISBN 978-1-84428-492-4

ISBN 978-1-84428-494-8

ISBN 978-1-84428-493-1

ISBN 978-0-7445-4067-3

ISBN 978-0-7445-7518-7

ISBN 978-0-7445-9408-9

ISBN 978-1-84428-541-9

Available from all good booksellers

www.walkerbooks.co.uk